REBELS

GHOST SHIP

STAR WARS

Rebel Fashion

ENTANGLEMENT

Based on the episode "Entanglement," written by Henry Gilroy and Simon Kinberg

Adapted by Brooke Vitale

© & TM 2014 Lucasfilm Ltd.

Printed in China

First Edition, December 2014
1 3 5 7 9 10 8 6 4 2

ISBN 978-1-4847-2611-2
T425-2382-5-14356

Visit the official *Star Wars* website at: www.starwars.com
This book was printed on paper created from a sustainable source.

Disney
LUCASFILM
PRESS

Los Angeles • New York

"Zeb! Where are you?" Kanan asked over his comlink.

Zeb looked around. Kanan had told Zeb to meet him in the alley, but no one was there. "I'm at the rendezvous point," Zeb answered. "Where are you?"

Zeb's comlink crackled. "You're not at the rendezvous point because *I'm* at the rendezvous point."

Zeb scratched his head. If Kanan was in the right place, where was *he*? "Uh, where's the rendezvous point again?" he asked.

Kanan sighed. "In the alley by the marketplace!"

Zeb looked around again. At least he was halfway right.
He was in *an* alley!

With a sigh, Zeb started forward to find the *right* alley.
He hadn't gone more than a few steps when he spotted two
stormtroopers surrounding a fruit vendor and his droid.

Zeb stopped to check out the situation.

"Don't hurt me," the vendor pleaded. "I am a friend."

"What? Is that a bribe?" said one of the stormtroopers.
"Well, now you're under arrest!"

Zeb watched the troopers, his anger growing. He had seen enough.

CRACK! Zeb slammed the stormtroopers' heads together and they dropped to the ground.

"So are you going to make the rendezvous or not?" Kanan asked over the comlink.

Before Zeb could answer, four more troopers raced into the alley.

"Hey! You! Stop!" they cried.

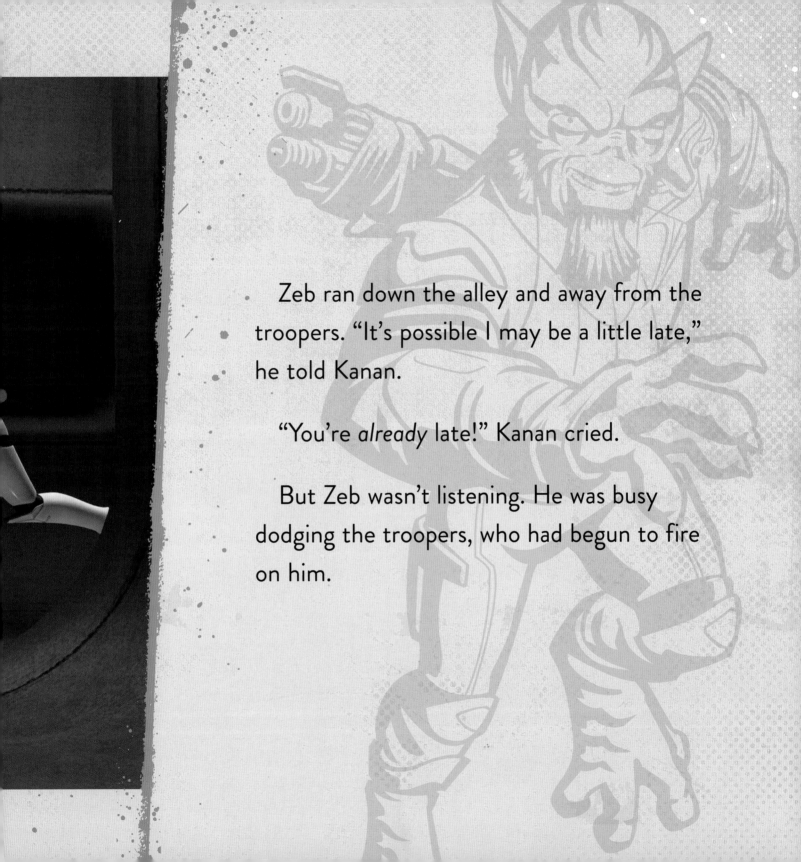

Zeb ran down the alley and away from the troopers. "It's possible I may be a little late," he told Kanan.

"You're *already* late!" Kanan cried.

But Zeb wasn't listening. He was busy dodging the troopers, who had begun to fire on him.

Zeb ducked around a corner and found himself on a TIE fighter landing pad. He quickly hid behind a wall. Seconds later, the four troopers emerged in front of him. They looked around, confused. Where was Zeb?

Zeb quietly stepped forward. Grabbing one of the stormtroopers, he swung him into the others. All four troopers fell down. As they did, one of their weapons went off.

"Zeb, what's going on?" Kanan called. "Wait . . . are you fighting stormtroopers?"

"What makes you say that?" Zeb asked with a grin.

As one of the troopers got to his feet, Zeb pulled out his bo-rifle. He turned on the stun function. Energy danced through the tip of the weapon.

"I heard blaster fire," Kanan said.

Zeb jabbed the trooper with his bo-rifle, and the stormtrooper cried out in pain.

"And screaming!" Kanan added.

"There may be more screaming," Zeb said as another stormtrooper rose to his feet. He bashed the trooper, who fell back in a heap of moans.

"Oh, that's great," Kanan said. "You get lost in the middle of a mission and decide to start your own battle. Again."

"Didn't decide. It just happened. This time," Zeb answered.

Just then, Zeb was interrupted by a TIE fighter pilot. The pilot aimed his blaster at Zeb. "LS-60-7, requesting reinforcements!" he called into his comlink.

But Zeb was too fast for the pilot. He jumped on top of the TIE fighter and yanked the pilot out of his seat.

"Zeb, are you embarrassing the Imperials again?" Kanan asked.

Zeb grinned. "Honestly, Kanan, it's hard not to," he answered.

Jumping down from the TIE fighter, Zeb found himself face-to-face with eight stormtroopers.

As the troopers blasted at him, Zeb rolled away and under the TIE fighter. Looking up, he noticed that the fuel was leaking.

Zeb scrambled away from the TIE fighter just as another blast hit it. The TIE fighter exploded.

"Zeb, I see smoke," Kanan called. "Was that . . . a TIE fighter exploding?"

"No," Zeb said, coughing. "Okay, yes."

"Nice!" Kanan congratulated him. "Okay, stay put. I'll follow the smoke and pick you up."

Brushing himself off, Zeb walked back toward the alley where the vendor and his droid stood. The vendor raced to his cart and began digging through it.

A moment later, the vendor came back. Holding up his hand, he offered Zeb his money as thanks. But Zeb didn't want the vendor's money. He was always up for a good fight—especially against the Empire!

Reaching past the vendor, Zeb picked up a single piece of fruit from the cart. He held it up. He would take the fruit as payment . . . if it was okay with the vendor.

The vendor nodded. He watched happily as Zeb took a bite of his fruit.

Just then, Zeb heard a noise in the alley. It was more stormtroopers. Tossing the rest of the fruit aside, he unslung his bo-rifle.

He was ready. . . .